OLIVIA
Leads a Parade

adapted by Kama Einhorn
based on the screenplay
written by Pat Resnick

illustrated by Shane L. Johnson

Simon Spotlight
New York   London   Toronto   Sydney

Based on the TV series *OLIVIA*™ as seen on Nickelodeon™

SIMON SPOTLIGHT
An imprint of Simon & Schuster Children's Publishing Division
1230 Avenue of the Americas, New York, New York 10020
Copyright © 2011 Silver Lining Productions Limited (a Chorion company).
All rights reserved. OLIVIA™ and © 2011 Ian Falconer. All rights reserved.
All rights reserved, including the right of reproduction in whole or in part in any form.
SIMON SPOTLIGHT and colophon are registered trademarks of Simon & Schuster, Inc.
For information about special discounts for bulk purchases, please contact Simon & Schuster Special Sales at
1-866-506-1949 or business@simonandschuster.com.
Manufactured in the United States of America 0611 LAK
3 4 5 6 7 8 9 10
ISBN 978-1-4424-2137-0

"Ah, nothing like watching a parade from the comfort of your own couch," said Olivia to her dad as they watched a parade on television.

"I want to play that huge drum!" said Julian.

"Look at the floats!" said Ian.

"And the majorettes!" Olivia added. "I'd like to be the one twirling the baton. . . ."

Olivia imagined herself as a marching majorette . . .
spinning her baton . . .
tossing it into the air . . .
twirling around . . .
and doing a split.
TA-DA!

"I wish we could have parades like that in our town," said Ian.
Olivia had a brilliant idea. "Ian, we can have our *own* parade!"
"Great!" said Julian and Ian.

They went right to work. "Julian, you can be the marching band," declared Olivia. "Ian, you can play the cymbals. And I'm the majorette—this ruler is my baton! Now, all together!"

Everyone began to march in place. *BAM, CRASH, BOOM!* went the parade band, and Perry howled along.

Upstairs, Olivia's mother was trying to get baby William to take his nap. She poked her head out of the window and called down, "Kids, could you play your music a little more quietly?"

"WHAT, MOM?" shouted Olivia.

"William needs his nap!" her mom answered.

"Oops. Sorry, Mom," Olivia and Ian said.

They went inside to look for things they could use in a quiet parade. Olivia found an old pennant from a baseball game.

"Pennants! Pennants are quiet," she said. She started making a pretty new pennant from the old one.

"Just needs a little glue," she said. "Perfect!"

But the glue stuck to Olivia's hand. "Uh-oh! It's stuck!" she said, and they all giggled.

Olivia ran into William's room, where her mom was still trying to get William to fall asleep.

"Mom, I need a little help!" Olivia said loudly.

William cried loudly. He had just fallen asleep, and now he was awake again.

"Olivia, I asked you to keep the noise down," her mother sighed. "Maybe he'd like some fresh air," she said. She picked William up to take him outside.

Olivia, Ian, and Julian went outside to try again.

"Okay, let's take it from the top!" Olivia announced. "Shhh, the cymbals are too loud, Ian. But can you do tricks on your tricycle?" she suggested. "Okay, parade, get ready to march! One, two, three, go!"

The three marched along proudly until Olivia's baton got stuck in the tree. Then Ian crashed his tricycle loudly into the garbage cans. This parade was not very quiet.

Just then, Francine and Alexandra came by. "What's making all that noise?" asked Francine.

"Shhh!" said Olivia. "Hi, Francine. Hi, Alexandra," she whispered. "We need to be quiet because my baby brother is trying to nap."

"What are you guys doing?" asked Alexandra.

"We're having a parade," said Julian. "Want to be in it?"

Francine seemed interested. "What kind of parade?"

"A fabulous parade," Olivia promised. "But we have to be very quiet."

"The parade will begin here," Olivia explained. "I'll be in the front twirling my baton. Julian will be leading the drummers here. Ian, you'll ride your tricycle here. Francine and Alexandra, you can pull the float back here."
Francine paused. "I think the parade should have clowns in it." She added a clown to the drawing.

"I'm not really a clown person," Olivia told Francine.

"Really?" Francine said. "Well, I'm a clown person! I'll lead my own parade. *With* clowns. Come on, Alexandra." And they left.

"Don't worry, our parade will be much better," Olivia reassured Julian and Ian.

Soon Olivia's mom came to say hello. William was wide-awake and squirmy.
"How are you kids doing?" she asked.
"Great," said Olivia. "Mom, you should take William for a drive," she
suggested. "He always falls asleep in the car."
"I wish I could," her mom said. "But I have too much work to catch up on. And
besides, I wouldn't want to miss the parade."

"Okay, let's decorate the float!" Olivia exclaimed. Francine and her friends decorated their float too, and Francine got into her clown costume.

Both parades marched along the sidewalk until they bumped right into each other.

"Excuse me, Olivia," Francine said. "My parade needs to get through."
"But we thought of the parade first," Olivia pointed out. Then she had an idea.

Olivia imagined a fabulous parade with all of her friends. Wouldn't one big parade be better than two medium-size parades?

"Come on, let's join parades!" Olivia said to Francine.

Francine thought about it and talked to her friends. "Okay," she agreed.

"But I'm not changing out of my clown costume."

"Okay, follow my lead everybody!" said Olivia.

Several people had already gathered on the sidewalk to watch the parade.
"Let the parade begin!" Olivia exclaimed loudly. Then she saw her mom
holding William.
"I have an idea! Can William ride in the parade too?" she asked her mom.
Her mom smiled and shrugged. "Why not? He's not sleeping anyway!"

Now Olivia was ready. "Follow my lead, everybody.
William says, 'Let the parade begin!'"
And it did.

It was a very noisy parade.
William fell asleep right away.
It was a wonderful parade.

"Thank you for getting William to sleep today," Olivia's mom said as she tucked her in. "It was a great parade."

Olivia yawned. "I think I'm only going to have a parade once every five years because they're so much work," she said sleepily. "No books tonight, Mom."

"Wow, you must really be tired," her mom said.

"I'll have double books tomorrow," Olivia reassured her. "Good night."

"Good night, Olivia."